For Toby,
whose alter ego 'Nicky Nude'
inspired the writing of this book. xx

A TEMPLAR BOOK

First published in the UK in 2013 by Templar Publishing,
an imprint of The Templar Company Limited,
Deepdene Lodge, Deepdene Avenue, Dorking, Surrey, RH5 4AT, UK
www.templarco.co.uk

First edition

ISBN 978-1-84877-323-3

Edited by Hannah Wilson

Printed in Malaysia

1112 006

NAKED TREVOR

Rebecca Elliott

templar publishing

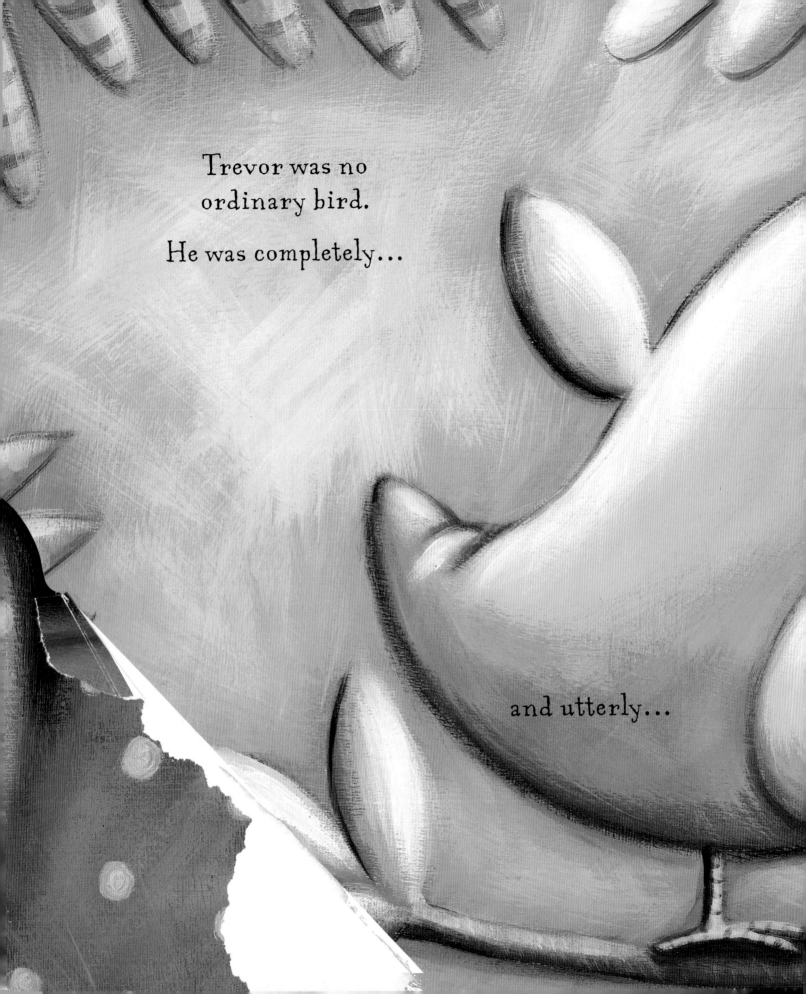

Trevor was no ordinary bird.

He was completely...

and utterly...

It's a well kept secret that all birds
are actually quite naked.

Every morning they put on their feathery clothes
and go about their day.

But Trevor refused to wear ANY outfit.

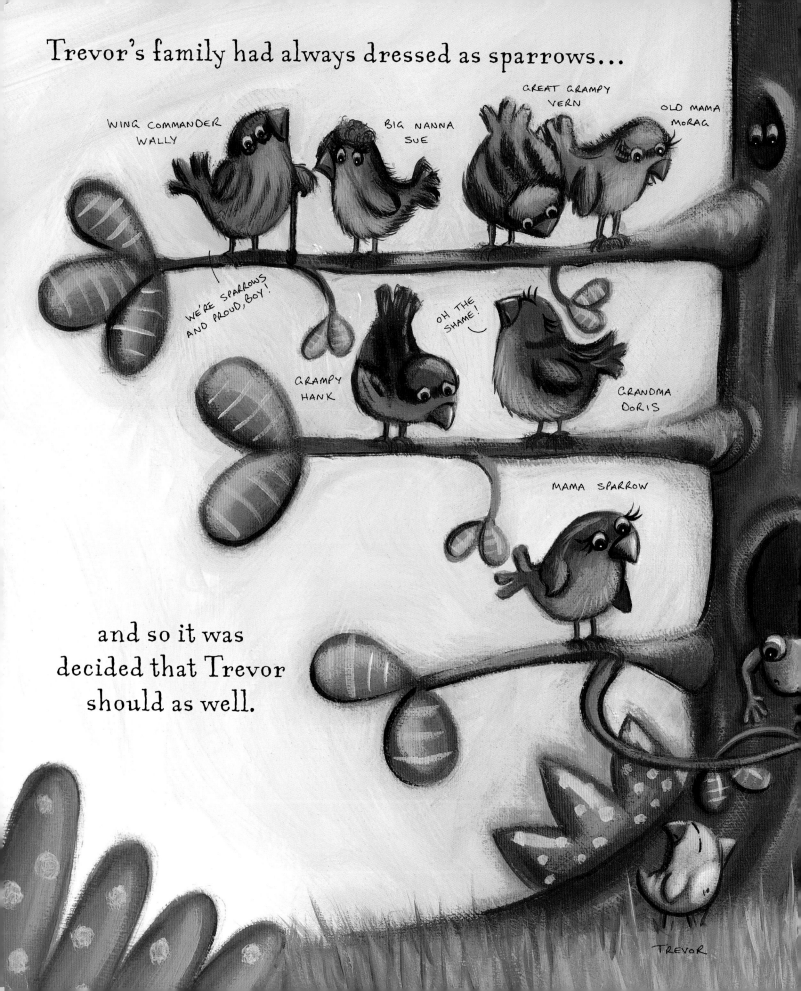

But Trevor didn't
want to be a sparrow.

"You must wear
your sparrow outfit!" they said.
"Never!" said Trevor.

Trevor wanted to find his own outfit. And so one morning he woke up very early and flew away from home.

But with no feathers on his naked wings,
Trevor wasn't very good at flying.

And so he flew...

He picked himself up
and carried on his journey.

UH-OH!

But the weight of the mud
on his naked body
meant he couldn't fly straight,
and he flew...

Again, he picked himself up
and carried on his journey.

WHOA!

But the weight of the mud on his naked body
and the leaves on his naked wings
brought him spiralling down and this time he flew...

straight into a patch of beautiful flowers.

FLOMP!

"This isn't going to work,"
he said sadly.

So he launched his muddy,
leafy, flowery,
naked body into the air
and flew back home.

"OK," said Trevor,

"I'm ready to wear
my sparrow clothes now."

But they all looked at him
and cried, "Never!"

"Why ever not?"
asked Trevor.

"Because you look FANTASTIC!" they all said.

Trevor looked down at his beautiful new outfit made of mud, leaves and flower petals, and he realised he wasn't a sparrow or a blackbird or a robin – he was a spectacular TREVOR!!

The others looked down at their
own boring outfits and threw them off.

And then everyone was naked.

EXCEPT for TREVOR!

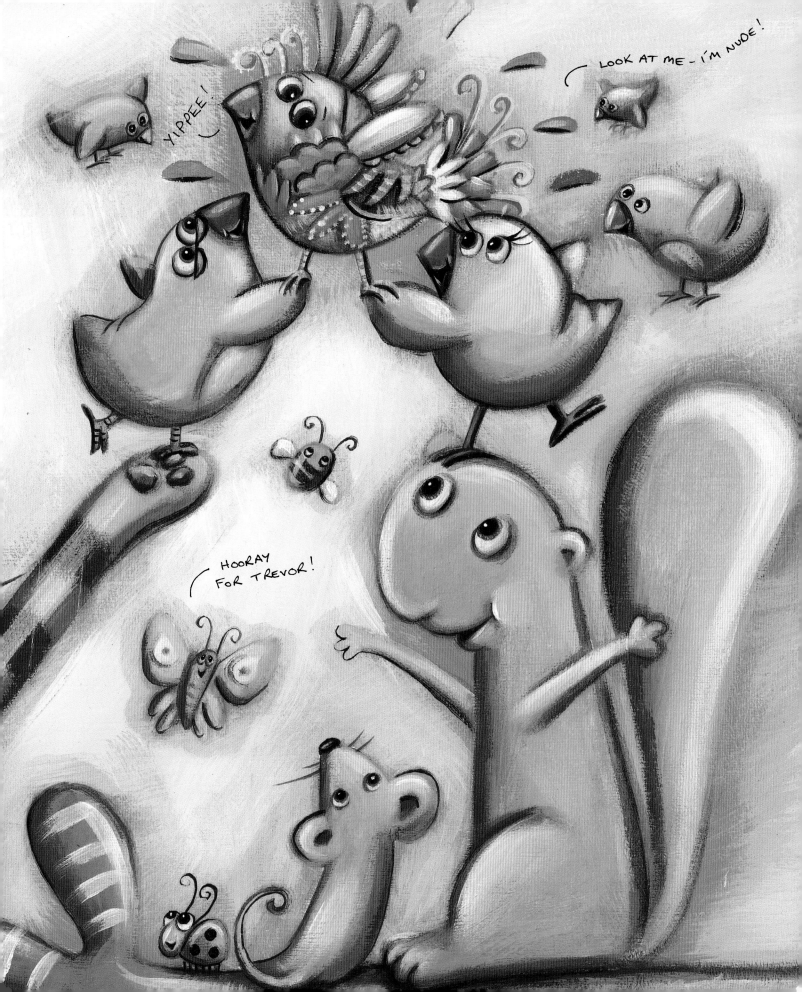

THE END